FOR ECON, WHO WENT . . .
AND HELPED INSPIRE THIS STORY —A. L.

FOR TERESA K. AND BRYNLEE —B. S.

BLOOMSBURY CHILDREN'S BOOKS
Bloomsbury Publishing Inc., part of Bloomsbury Publishing Plc
1385 Broadway, New York, NY 10018

BLOOMSBURY, BLOOMSBURY CHILDREN'S BOOKS, and the Diana logo are trademarks of Bloomsbury Publishing Plc

First published in the United States of America in June 2020 by Bloomsbury Children's Books

Text copyright © 2020 by Adam Lehrhaupt • Illustrations copyright © 2020 by Benson Shum

Bloomsbury books may be purchased for business or promotional use. For information on bulk purchases please contact
Macmillan Corporate and Premium Sales Department at specialmarkets@macmillan.com

Library of Congress Cataloging-in-Publication Data
Names: Lehrhaupt, Adam, author. | Shum, Benson, illustrator.
Title: Sloth went / by Adam Lehrhaupt ; illustrated by Benson Shum.
Description: New York : Bloomsbury Children's Books, 2020.
Summary: With encouragement from his mother and animal friends, a nervous young Sloth makes his first,
dangerous climb down the tree to take care of important business. Includes facts about sloths and how they "poop."
Identifiers: LCCN 2019023411 (print) | LCCN 2019023412 (e-book)
ISBN 978-1-5476-0245-2 (hardcover) • ISBN 978-1-5476-0246-9 (e-book) • ISBN 978-1-5476-0247-6 (e-PDF)
Subjects: CYAC: Defecation—Fiction. | Sloths—Fiction. | Jungle animals—Fiction.
Classification: LCC PZ7.L532745 Slo 2020 (print) | LCC PZ7.L532745 (e-book) | DDC [E]—dc23
LC record available at https://lccn.loc.gov/2019023411

Art created with watercolor and ink • Typeset in Sassoon Sans Slope Std • Book design by Danielle Ceccolini
Printed in China by Leo Paper Products, Heshan, Guangdong
2 4 6 8 10 9 7 5 3 1

All papers used by Bloomsbury Publishing Plc are natural, recyclable products made from wood grown in well-managed forests.
The manufacturing processes conform to the environmental regulations of the country of origin.

To find out more about our authors and books visit www.bloomsbury.com and sign up for our newsletters.

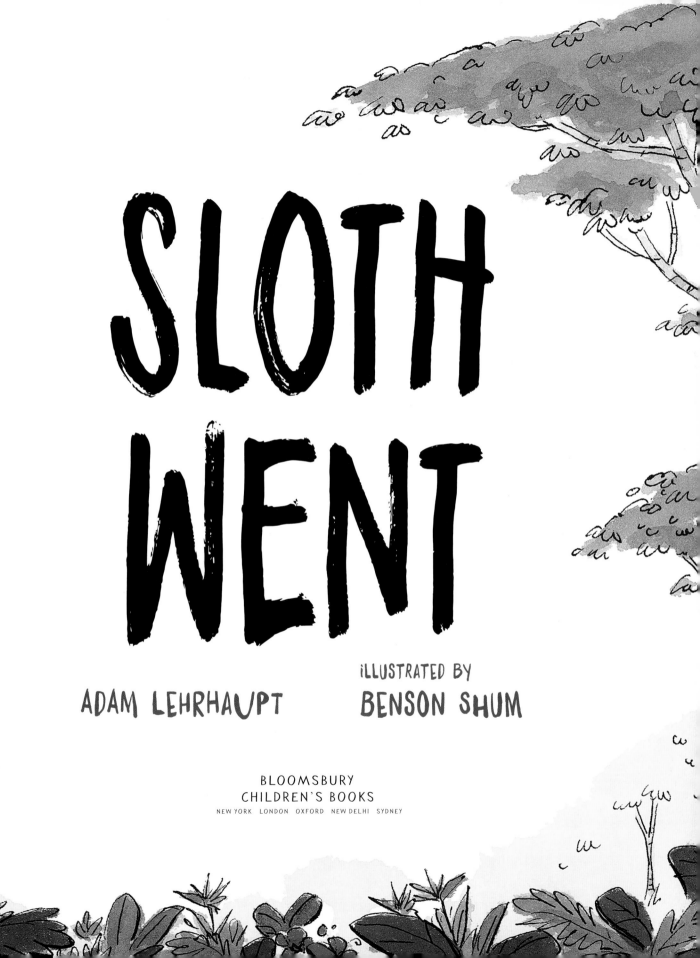

SLOTH WENT

ADAM LEHRHAUPT

ILLUSTRATED BY
BENSON SHUM

BLOOMSBURY
CHILDREN'S BOOKS
NEW YORK LONDON OXFORD NEW DELHI SYDNEY

It was Sloth's big day.

He was excited.

And nervous.

"What if something happens?" he asked.
"What if *nothing* happens?"

Momma knew Sloth was ready.

"Don't worry," she said. "Everything will come out fine."

"But what if I don't make it?" Sloth asked.

"You'll make it," Momma said. "And when you get back, I'll have a surprise."

"A surprise?" Sloth asked.
"Okay. I'll go."

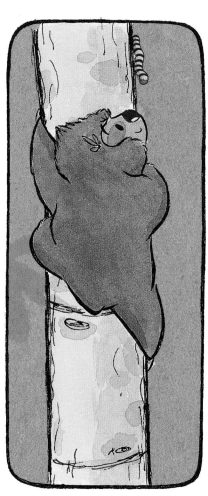

Sloth went.

"It's your big day,"
Butterfly said. "How's it going?"

"I don't think I'm gonna
make it," Sloth grumbled.

"It's okay if you don't,"
said Butterfly.

"It is?" asked Sloth.

"Of course!" Butterfly said. "As long as you keep trying."

"I will," Sloth promised.

So he did.

"Big day today," Frog said.
"We're all rooting for you."

"I'm not gonna make it,"
Sloth pouted.

"Just listen to your body and it will all work out," Frog said.

What *was* his body telling him?
"Maybe I *can* make it," Sloth said.

He scanned the ground.
He saw the *perfect* spot.

Sloth climbed down . . .
and made a dash for it.

Sloths can dash quickly
when they really need to go.

Sloth settled in to take care of business.

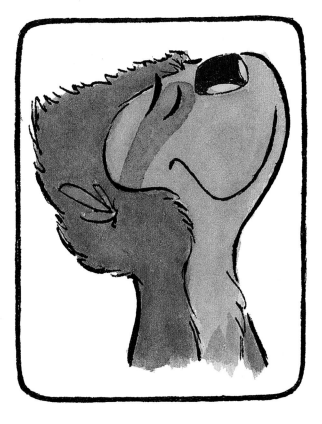

"I did it!" Sloth cheered.

Sloth started back up his tree.
He couldn't wait to tell everyone.

THE *REAL* SLOTH POOP ADVENTURE

Tree-dwelling sloths lead a very chill lifestyle, with little movement throughout the day. They're so relaxed that it can take up to a MONTH to digest a meal. A whole month! Can you believe that?

With such slow digestion, sloths only need to poop about once a week. Seems like that would make potty training easy, right? But sometimes they experience problems when making a slothy poo. It can be very *hard* to go. Sound familiar?

And that's not all. Sloths need to descend to the forest floor before they can poop. Scientists don't know why sloths make this dangerous trek. They must benefit from this potty-time journey to the ground in some way, because sloths risk their lives making the trip. Can you guess why it's so dangerous?

On the ground, slow-moving sloths are closer to many scary predators. Kind of makes using your own toilet seem cozy by comparison, doesn't it? I mean, there's no jaguar in your potty, is there?

Once they reach the forest floor, sloths do a special "poop dance" to create a hole in the ground with their tail. Then, they use the hole as a potty.

And, because their poop is a whole week's worth, their poops can be big! They drop up to 33 percent of their body weight in just one poo. *Ouch!* I'm sure sloths understand why potty training can be a tough time for us, too.

After they finish, sloths do another dance to cover up the poop. So polite! Finally, they begin the long, dangerous climb back up their tree, only to repeat this process the next week.

Wow! I'm glad I'm not a sloth. But I tell you what, next time I poop, I'm gonna try that dance. It sounds like fun!